SCHOLASTIC PRESS
NEW YORK

Library of Congress Cataloging-in-Publication Data
Swim! Swim! / by Lerch. — 1st ed.   p. cm.
Summary: Lerch the fish is lonely, and after trying to befriend some unreceptive—
and inanimate—objects, he finally succeeds in finding a friend.
ISBN 978-0-545-09419-1
[1. Fishes—Fiction. 2. Friendship—Fiction.]
PZ7.S981 2010   [E]—dc22   2009020520
10 9 8 7 6 5 4 3 2 1   10 11 12 13 14

Printed in Singapore   46
First edition, July 2010

The text was hand-lettered by Lerch.
The illustrations were done in ink and Photoshop.

Book design by Becky Terhune

SO, YOU ARE NOT TALKING.
FINE. BE THAT WAY. THIS IS A BIG WORLD. I'LL FIND A FRIEND.

CHILDREN'S ROOM

I'LL TRY TALKING BUBBLE.
BLUB BLUB BLUB BLUB BLUB BLUB BLUB BLUB BLUB BLUB BLUB BLUB BLUB BLUB BLUB BLUB BLUB BLUB BLUB BLUB BLUB BLUB BLUB BLUB BLUB BLUB BLUB BLUB BLUB BLUB BLUB BLUB BLUB BLUB BLUB BLUB BLUB BLUB BLUB BLUB BLUB BLUB BLUB BLUB BLUB BLUB BLUB BLUB BLUB BLUB BLUB!

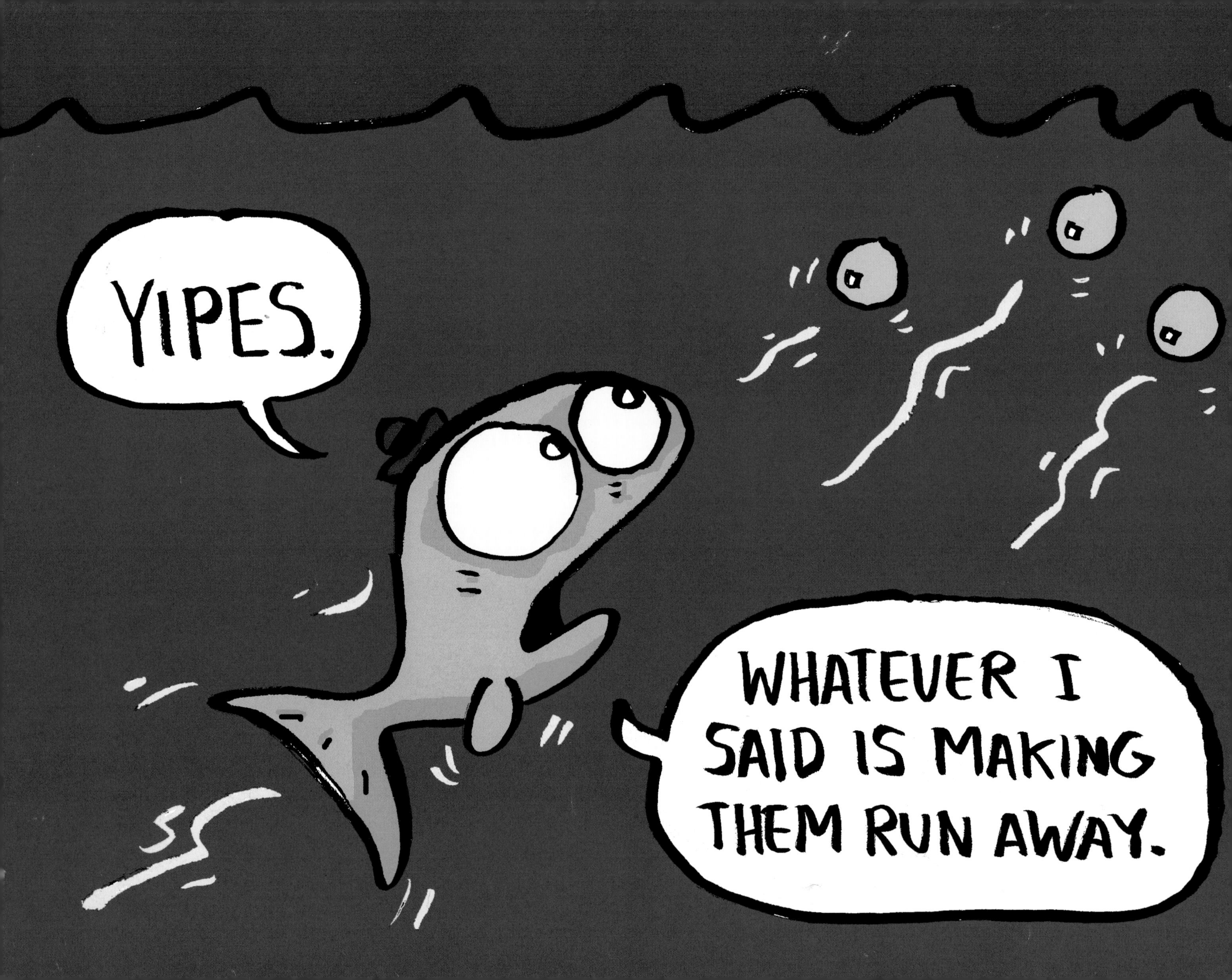
YIPES.
WHATEVER I SAID IS MAKING THEM RUN AWAY.

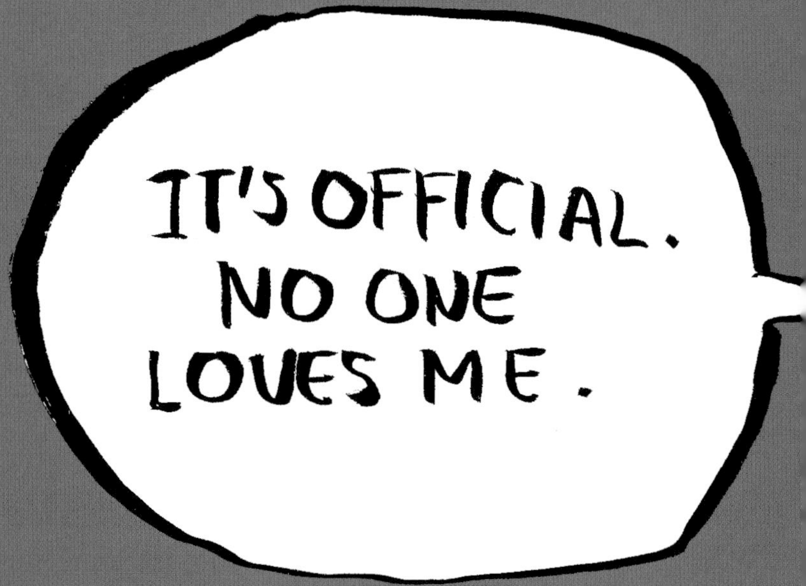
IT'S OFFICIAL. NO ONE LOVES ME.

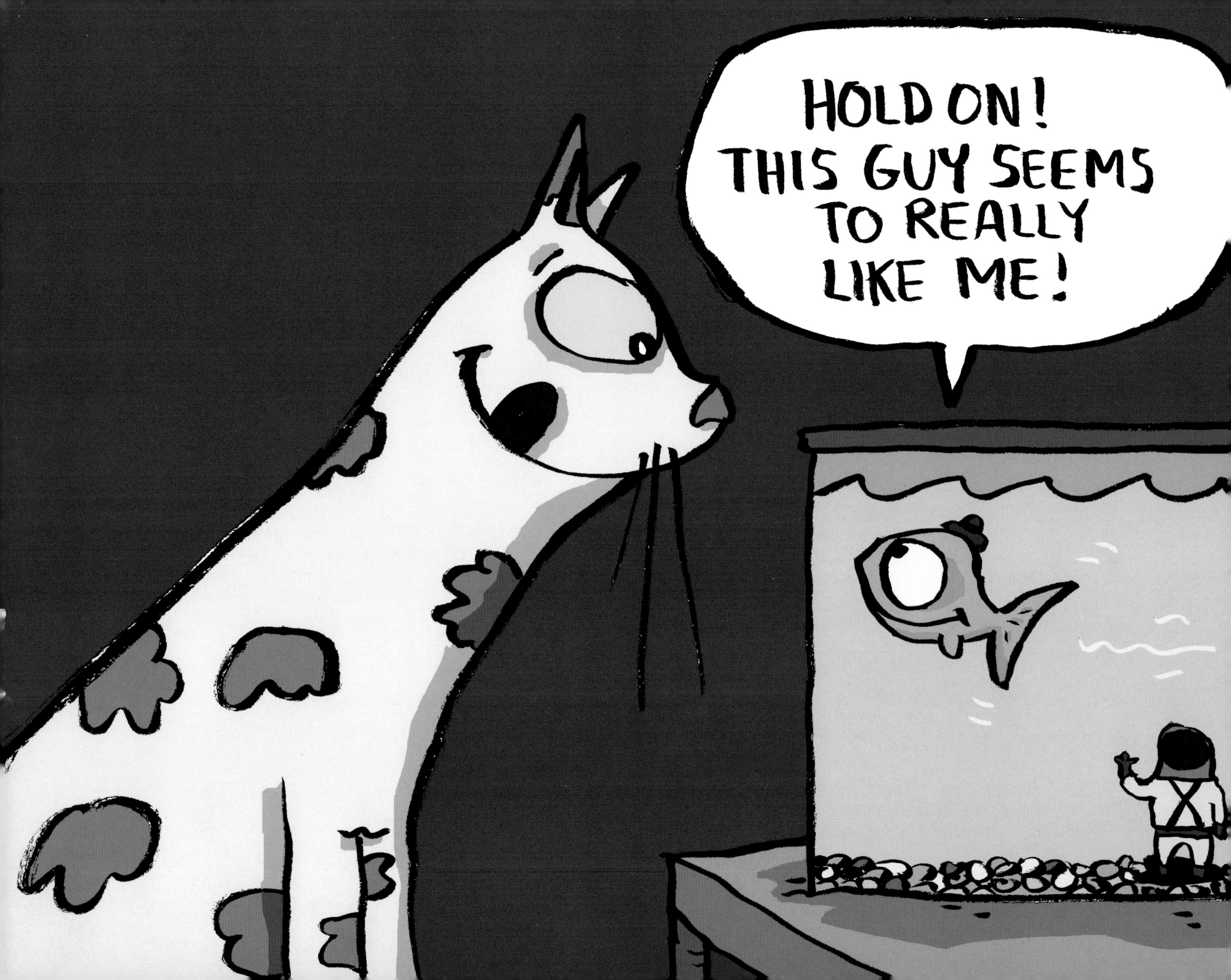
HOLD ON! THIS GUY SEEMS TO REALLY LIKE ME!